THE DOORMAN

by EDWARD GRIMM   *pictures by* TED LEWIN

ORCHARD BOOKS • NEW YORK

Text copyright © 2000 by Edward Grimm
Illustrations copyright © 2000 by Ted Lewin

Orchard Books, A Grolier Company
95 Madison Avenue, New York, NY 10016

Manufactured in the United States of America
Printed and bound by Phoenix Color Corp.
Book design by Mina Greenstein
The text of this book is set in 14 point Berling
Roman. The illustrations are watercolor.

10 9 8 7 6 5 4 3 2 1

Library of Congress Cataloging-in-Publication Data
Grimm, Edward.
The doorman / by Edward Grimm ;
pictures by Ted Lewin.   p.   cm.
Summary: A day in the life of a very special doorman
and the apartment tenants who are so fond of him.
ISBN 0-531-30280-6 (trade)
ISBN 0-531-33280-2 (library)
[1. Apartment houses—Fiction.] I. Lewin, Ted, ill.
II. Title.
PZ7.G88435 Do 2000 [E]—dc21
99-54160

APR 14 '0?

JOHN sipped his coffee. It made his stomach feel as warm as a fireplace. Even on a cold winter morning like this one, he loved coming to work at the big apartment house. He felt responsible for everyone who lived there—as if he were the captain of a ship.

He liked the people who lived in the building. They were all different. There was Mrs. Ferguson, who went down to the laundry room with her parrot on her shoulder. And Mr. Davis, who almost never went outside but always wanted to talk about the weather anyway.

Most of all, John liked the old people and the children. That was because they were the ones he could do the most for.

John looked at his watch. Seven-thirty. Time to get ready. He fastened the brass buttons of his jacket and fixed his hat at just the right angle.

Here they came!

First, as always, was Mr. Ramirez, who went jogging every morning. Because it was windy, he had a scarf around his neck. "How many miles today?" John asked him.

Mr. Ramirez held up three fingers and ducked out into the cold air.

Next were the Jackson twins, off to their play group in their puffy
winter snowsuits. "Hi, John," they said together.
   He gave them a rough hug. "Mornin', fellas."

Soon a parade of people came through the lobby, heading for work and school with briefcases, books, and backpacks. "You have a good day now," John told them all.

"You, too, John," they all said.

Nellie Harrigan bounced into the lobby. "Now, let me see. What was I supposed to remember about today?" John said, taking off his hat and scratching his head.

"It's my birthday!" Nellie shouted, dancing around him.

"I know," said John, "and you're having a party." But Nellie was already out the door.

Right behind her came Mrs. Klein. She was going to the doctor to find out how her broken arm was healing. John helped her button her coat, then hurried her past the icy wind and into a taxicab.

The wind seemed to push the morning along, and soon it was time for lunch. John made himself a cup of tea on the hot plate in the basement and ate the tuna fish sandwich and apple his wife had packed for him.

Early in the afternoon the mailman arrived. He plopped envelopes into the long rows of metal mailboxes at the back of the lobby. John took the packages that wouldn't fit and put them away for safekeeping until people came home.

"Oh, John, they told me my arm is healing beautifully," Mrs. Klein said when she came back from the doctor.

"That's great," John said, helping her into the elevator and pressing the button for her floor. "You take good care now."

Mrs. Klein blew him a little kiss.

Now the children began returning from school. They loved to play tricks on John, like breathing on the front doors he had just cleaned. They left little ghosts of themselves on the glass. He chased them around the lobby, and they laughed as hard as they ran.

"Look, John," said Nellie Harrigan, showing him her present. "Goldfish!"

"Aren't they something!" John said. "You take good care of them now."

"I will," said Nellie and promised to save him some of her birthday cake.

Suddenly everything seemed to be happening at once. The cake for Nellie's party came. Then her friends started to arrive. They had so many balloons it seemed as if the elevator would take off clear into the sky.

The plumbers came to fix a leak, hurrying through the lobby with their tools and equipment. There were deliveries of groceries, prescriptions from the pharmacy, and clothes from the dry cleaner.

A TV repairman arrived with a big coil of cable over his shoulder like a pet snake. The painters left for the day with their ladders and cans. They looked tired, and some of them had little flecks of paint on their eyebrows.

John was in the middle of it all, like a policeman in a big, busy traffic circle.

Before John knew it, Bill, the doorman who worked the next shift, arrived. While John was telling him about what had happened during the day, the elevator door opened. Nellie's party was over. As soon as the children streamed out the door, the wind made punching bags out of their balloons.

After Nellie came down with two pink-and-white wedges of birthday cake, John took a last look around. Already lots of lights were on in the windows. The building seemed strong and safe. He said good-night to Bill and left for home.

The next morning, instead of John, Bill was in the lobby. He told everyone the terrible news. On his way home, John had had a heart attack. He had died in the hospital with his family all around his bed.

No one could believe it. Mr. Ramirez didn't want to run that morning. The Jackson twins missed their hug. Mr. Davis said he didn't care what the weather was going to be. Nellie and Mrs. Klein couldn't seem to say anything. Even Mrs. Ferguson's parrot looked sad.

"It's a shame that John had such a bad heart," Bill said to Nellie.

"He did *not*," she said, stamping her foot. "He had a *good* heart."

Bill patted her shoulder. "You're right, Nellie. He had a really good heart. What I meant was that it wasn't strong enough."

Before she left for school, Nellie asked Bill for a favor. She had always wanted to try on John's hat. Could she do it just once? Bill smiled. "Sure, Nellie." He took the hat off the shelf where John's uniform was hanging. "Here."

Nellie put on John's hat and looked at herself in the mirror. The hat came down over her ears, but she didn't feel at all silly. Her eyes shining, she turned to Bill and said, "You have a good day now."

Nobody in the big apartment house ever forgot John. Memories of him stayed as fresh as the wind after a springtime shower.

As for Bill, he always remembered what John had said about making everybody in the building feel safe and happy.

That's why he paid extra attention to the old people. And that's why he let the children play tricks on him when they came home from school.

Like breathing on the front doors he had just cleaned. And leaving little ghosts of themselves on the glass.